For Patrick Hickey. J.W.
To Alison, Tim and their friendly Bear. T.R.

First published in Great Britain in 2013 by Andersen Press Ltd.,
20 Vauxhall Bridge Road, London SW1V 2SA.
Published in Australia by Random House Australia Pty.,
Level 3, 100 Pacific Highway, North Sydney, NSW 2060.
Text copyright © Jeanne Willis, 2013.
Illustrations copyright © Tony Ross, 2013.
The rights of Jeanne Willis and Tony Ross to be identified as the author
and illustrator of this work have been asserted by them in accordance
with the Copyright, Designs and Patents Act, 1988. All rights reserved.
Colour separated in Switzerland by Photolitho AG, Zürich.
Printed and bound in Malaysia by Tien Wah Press.
Tony Ross has used pen, ink and watercolour in this book.

10   9   8   7   6   5   4   3   2   1

British Library Cataloguing in Publication Data available.

ISBN 978 1 84939 512 0

This book has been printed on acid-free paper

Prince Charmless

Jeanne Willis & Tony Ross

Andersen Press

Since the day he was born, nothing was good enough
for Prince Charmless.
"I want to be a panda, not a prince!" he wailed.

"I want to live in a big, gold palace!" he cried. "Not this silly little *silver* one! There isn't enough room to swing an elephant!"

From the moment he woke until the time he went to bed,
he complained.
"I want to get up in the night, not the morning!"
he moaned to the maid.

At breakfast time, he shrieked at the cook, "I don't want toasted soldiers! I want toasted sailors!"

He had a right royal go at the butler.
"I want my ruby robe and emerald crown not my emerald robe and ruby crown!"

It was time for his daily ride around the palace gardens.
"Your carriage awaits, Your Majesty," said the chauffeur.
The prince's face fell.
"I'm not getting in that old banger. Fetch me a golden carriage!"

The chauffeur returned with a magnificent carriage pulled
by six shiny stallions, but Prince Charmless still wasn't happy.
"I don't want those old donkeys, I want six white unicorns!"

The chauffeur did his best but **Prince Charmless** was still unhappy.

As soon as he got home, he picked on the nanny.
He had every toy a child could want, but he still wasn't satisfied.
"You are a dull playmate, Nanny," he scolded. "I want my own jester!"

A jester arrived but Prince Charmless was not amused.
"Stop slapping me with a wet fish," he commanded. "I shan't
laugh until you use a mermaid."
"Odds bodikins! I'm leaving!" said the jester.

"So are we!" said the maid, the butler, the cook, the chauffeur and the nanny.
"Whatever shall we do?" sighed the queen.

"Call the magician!" said the king. But the magician had vanished in a puff of smoke.
"We can't rule the country and look after Prince Charming all on our own," said the queen.
"Maybe it's time he learnt to do things for himself," said the king.

The next morning, there was no maid to wake Prince Charmless,
so he had to get himself up.
He'd never seen the sun rise before, but instead of complaining,
he was pleased to see it was the same colours he'd have chosen himself.

There was no cook, so Prince Charmless had to make his own breakfast. He'd always hated cook's cornflakes, but when he poured the milk on all by himself, they tasted surprisingly delicious.

There was no butler, so Prince Charming had to dress himself. He'd always refused to tie his own shoes, but he was thrilled to learn he could knot his laces.

It was time for his ride around the gardens, but as there was no chauffeur, he had to walk.

Usually he'd have stamped and screamed, but he found to his joy that if he walked, he could travel wherever he pleased. He could go as slowly as he liked . . .

. . . or as fast!

He ran wild in the garden.

There was no one to bring lunch, so he climbed a tree
and picked an apple.
Somehow, it tasted better than the grandest of feasts.

Nanny wasn't there to organize games, so for once
he had to make up his own. He entertained himself for hours
and had much more fun than he did with the court jester.

Tired but happy, Prince Charmless went home and got into his pyjamas all by himself. When the king asked if he'd had a good day, he had absolutely no complaints.

When the queen went to kiss him goodnight, he was a completely different child – he was Prince Charming.

And for ever after that, he lived up to his new name . . .

... well, *most* of the time, at least.